W9-AOU-505

WHERE IS GRANDMA?

PETER SCHÖSSOW

WHERE IS GRANDMA?

My Trip to the Hospital

GECKO PRESS

We’re going to the hospital to see my grandma.
Gulsa is with me. She’s my nanny. Her name means “happy rose” in Kurdish.
Natasha, Shelley and Johanna are my nannies too, but today it’s Happy Rose. We’ve known each other since I was a baby. Which was ages ago.
Gulsa has been telling me about her new phone. You can do lots on it: watch movies, listen to music, play games, all kinds of things…

We're almost there.
Gulsa answers her phone.
It's Corinna. They talk and talk about someone who did this, and someone else who said that… I'm bored.
I want to see Grandma.

"I'll be inside," I tell Gulsa.
"All right," says Gulsa. "But don't go far…"
OMEGA

CLINIC

It’s busy and noisy—like at the airport.
I look around.
Lots of people. No sign of Grandma.
At the back there’s a sign with a small i.
I know you can ask for help there.
I walk over to the desk.

01

"Hello!" I say to the lady under the **i**.

"Hello, young man. What can I do for you?"

"I'm here to see Grandma."

"Where is your grandma?"

"In bed."

"And why is that?"

"She's not well."

"What's her name?"

"We call her Grandma."

"Right…" says the lady under the **i**. "We don't seem to be getting very far. Are you here on your own?"

"No," I say. "I'm with Gulsa, but she's outside talking to Corinna. On her new phone."

"In that case, the best thing is to take a seat over there. And when Elsa arrives, we'll try again—maybe she can tell me more about your grandma."

"Gulsa. Her name is Gulsa."

"Gulsa. Right… Gulsa."

"Gulsa is Kurdish. Her name means happy rose."

"Uh-huh…"

GIVE
GIVE
THANK
Information

GIVE LIFE!
GIVE BLOOD!
THANK YOU!!!!
GIVE LIFE!
GIVE BLOOD!
THANK YOU!!!!

Luckily there's a seat for me.
I wait for Gulsa.
I can see her through the window.
She's still talking.
I'm still waiting.
Someone's giving out balloons. Should I ask for one? No, balloons are for babies.
Gulsa looks cross about something. This could take a while.
I keep waiting.
Gulsa keeps talking.
I'm bored. Really bored.
I'm going to look for Grandma.
Gulsa can come when she's ready.
GIVE LIFE!
GIVE BLOOD!
THANK YOU!!!!

Where shall I start?
This looks promising: long corridor, lots of doors.
I knock on all of them but no one answers.

More doors.

First door: I knock, no answer.

I try the door. It's locked.

Next door: I knock and someone calls, "Hang on, I'm coming!"

I wait a moment, and the door opens.

A man asks if he can help.

I tell him about Gulsa and her new phone, and Grandma. The man says he's sorry but he can't help.

I think *drat!* but say, "Thank you."

Third door: I knock, no answer. I try the handle.

Yes!

But the room is empty. On I go.

Door four: no answer. I try the handle.

Locked!

In the corridor three grown-ups are chatting.
"Do you know the five big lies that doctors tell?"
"Let's hear it!"
"First lie: You won't feel a thing! Second lie: This won't take long. Third lie: I'll be right back. Fourth lie: I've done this hundreds of times. Fifth lie: You're going to be just fine."
The grown-ups chuckle.
Hmm, I think. "Is that true?" I ask.
"He was telling a joke," says the woman, "but there's a grain of truth in it."
None of them knows where Grandma is.

08

Straight ahead there's a man in a wheelchair, wrapped in bandages like a mummy.
"What happened to you?" I ask.
"None of your business," he mumbles. He doesn't sound friendly.
"True," I say. "I was only asking."
I step away, but the mummy mumbles again: "I was meeting friends in town. There wasn't much time and I had to hurry. I ran across the road, along came a bus, and bang! They brought me here, lights and sirens all the way."
"In an ambulance?"
"An ambulance!"
"That's no good!"
"You can say that again! It hurts all over. And Vladimir and Estragon are probably still waiting for me, wondering what's happened. Most likely they'll get into trouble and who knows—"
"Hope for the best—that's what my grandma says. I'm on my way to see her. Get well soon!"
"Thanks!"

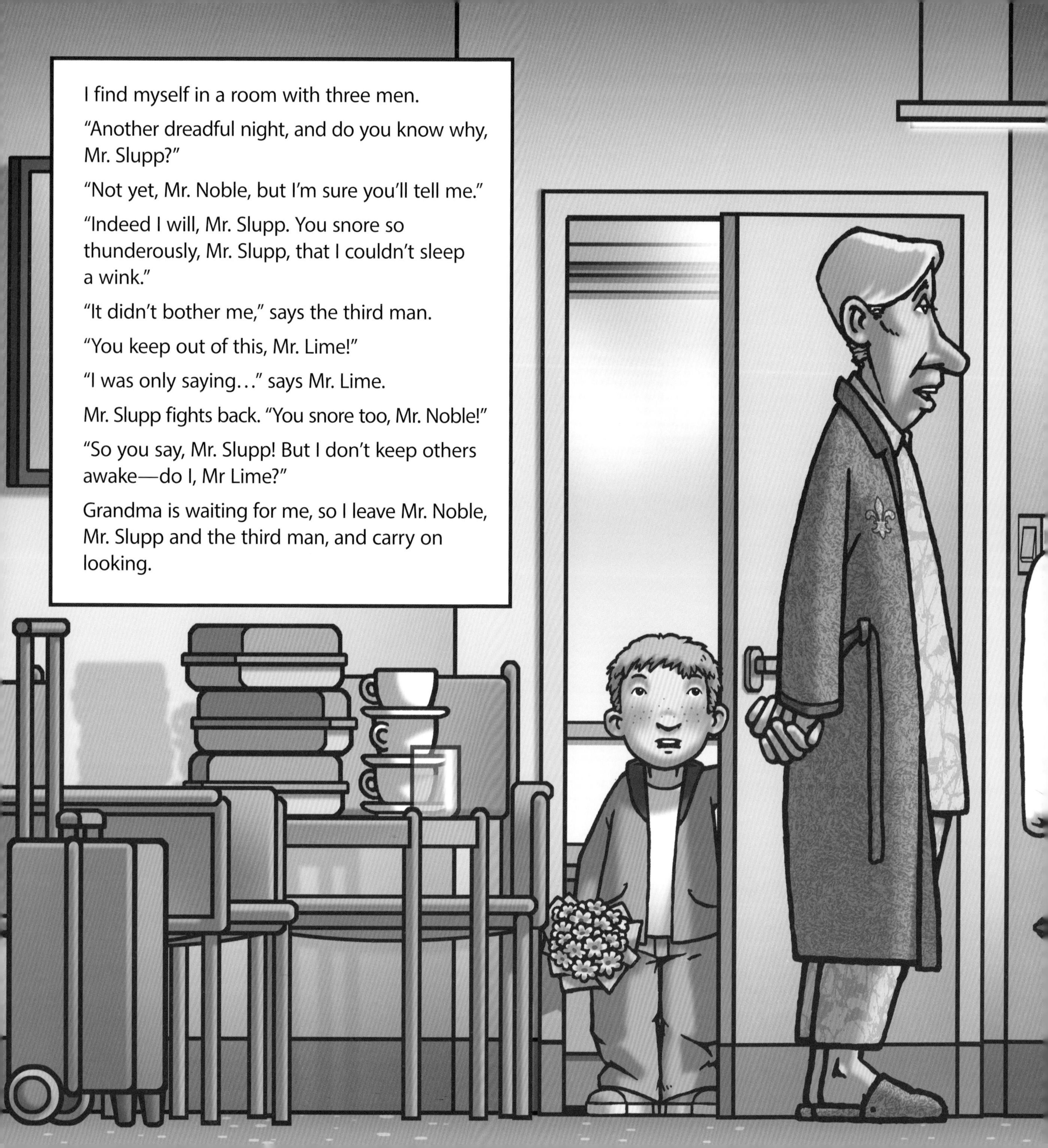

I find myself in a room with three men.

"Another dreadful night, and do you know why, Mr. Slupp?"

"Not yet, Mr. Noble, but I'm sure you'll tell me."

"Indeed I will, Mr. Slupp. You snore so thunderously, Mr. Slupp, that I couldn't sleep a wink."

"It didn't bother me," says the third man.

"You keep out of this, Mr. Lime!"

"I was only saying…" says Mr. Lime.

Mr. Slupp fights back. "You snore too, Mr. Noble!"

"So you say, Mr. Slupp! But I don't keep others awake—do I, Mr Lime?"

Grandma is waiting for me, so I leave Mr. Noble, Mr. Slupp and the third man, and carry on looking.

Wow, hospitals are big.

08
07

Enormous! How am I supposed to find Grandma?

25

28

Maybe I should've waited for Gulsa.
25
26
27
28
25
26
27
28
25
26
27
28

30
30
30

"Here to see your girlfriend?" says the guy in the corridor.
A real joker.
"I like your hat," I tell him.
"Chemo," he says.
"What's that?" I ask.
"It's when you get cancer. They pump you full of medicine. It makes you vomit, and your hair falls out. But if it works, it kills the bad cells and you get better."
"You know a lot!"
"I ask tons of questions. I need to know what they're doing to me, right?"
"And they just tell you?"
"They have to!"
"Will your hair grow back?"
"Eventually… Anyway, say hi to your girlfriend from me."
"My grandma!"
"Sure…say hi to your grandma!"

Hmm, this looks interesting! Those guys are from our football club, F.C.
The manager is in trouble.
"Are you crazy, Mr. Munchberger? You can't eat that! You might as well eat poison! You're on a diet!"

FCB

I call the elevator and get in. It goes up.

Drat! I wanted to go down.

"What's the matter with you, George? I've been looking for you everywhere, and now you ignore me."

I look around, but it's just me and the woman in the elevator. She must be talking to me.

"George! You shouldn't tease your poor mother." She glares.

"I'm not George. I'm Henry. And you're not my mother. She's working at home on the computer and we're not allowed to disturb her. I'm here with Gulsa. We're visiting my grandma."

The woman looks angry. "George, stop it right now! The joke's gone far enough!"

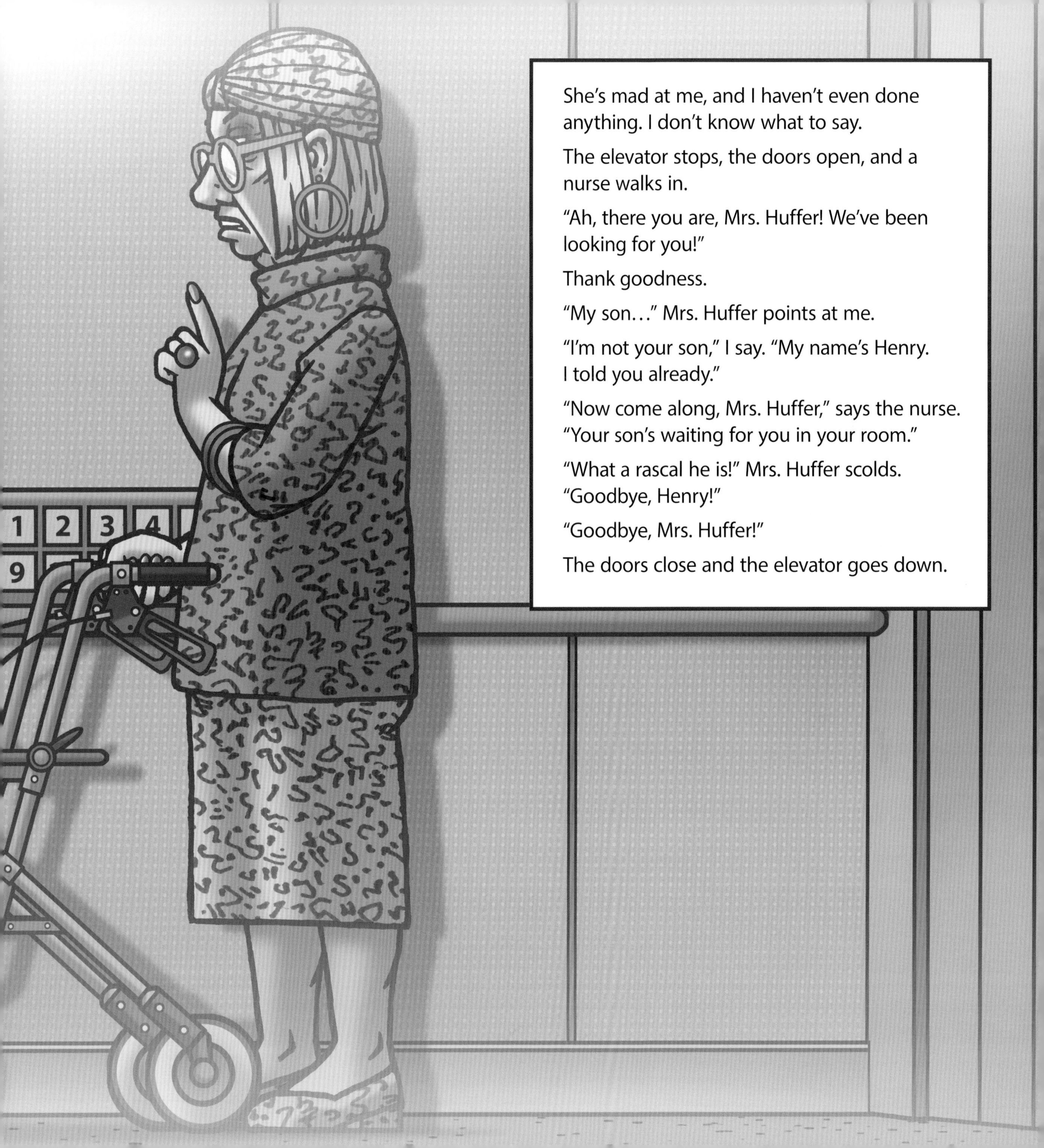

She's mad at me, and I haven't even done anything. I don't know what to say.

The elevator stops, the doors open, and a nurse walks in.

"Ah, there you are, Mrs. Huffer! We've been looking for you!"

Thank goodness.

"My son…" Mrs. Huffer points at me.

"I'm not your son," I say. "My name's Henry. I told you already."

"Now come along, Mrs. Huffer," says the nurse. "Your son's waiting for you in your room."

"What a rascal he is!" Mrs. Huffer scolds. "Goodbye, Henry!"

"Goodbye, Mrs. Huffer!"

The doors close and the elevator goes down.

Three people are in a waiting room.
"I'm looking for my grandma," I tell them. "Is she in there?"
The man says: "I didn't notice."
The woman says: "Sorry, I don't know. I've been reading."

And the newspaper says: “No, you won’t find her in there.”
“How do you know?”
“My wife’s in there—and she’s not your grandma.”
“You’re right,” I say. “Thank you!”
Please register at reception
The Daily Times

Another long corridor with lots of doors. There are people in the rooms. Even a few grandmas. But not mine.

02

Another ward.
“I was wondering if my grandma is here.”
“Well, this is the maternity ward. We’ve got mothers and babies, but no grandmas—unless…” She checks her computer. “No, there aren’t any visitors right now.”
Drat!
Maternity
Reception
Obstetrics

Before I can ask to see the new little babies, one comes along.
Babies are so cute when they're stretching, pulling faces, burping, looking around.
But not when they're screaming. Or making terrible smells. That's not cute at all.
NO ENTRY

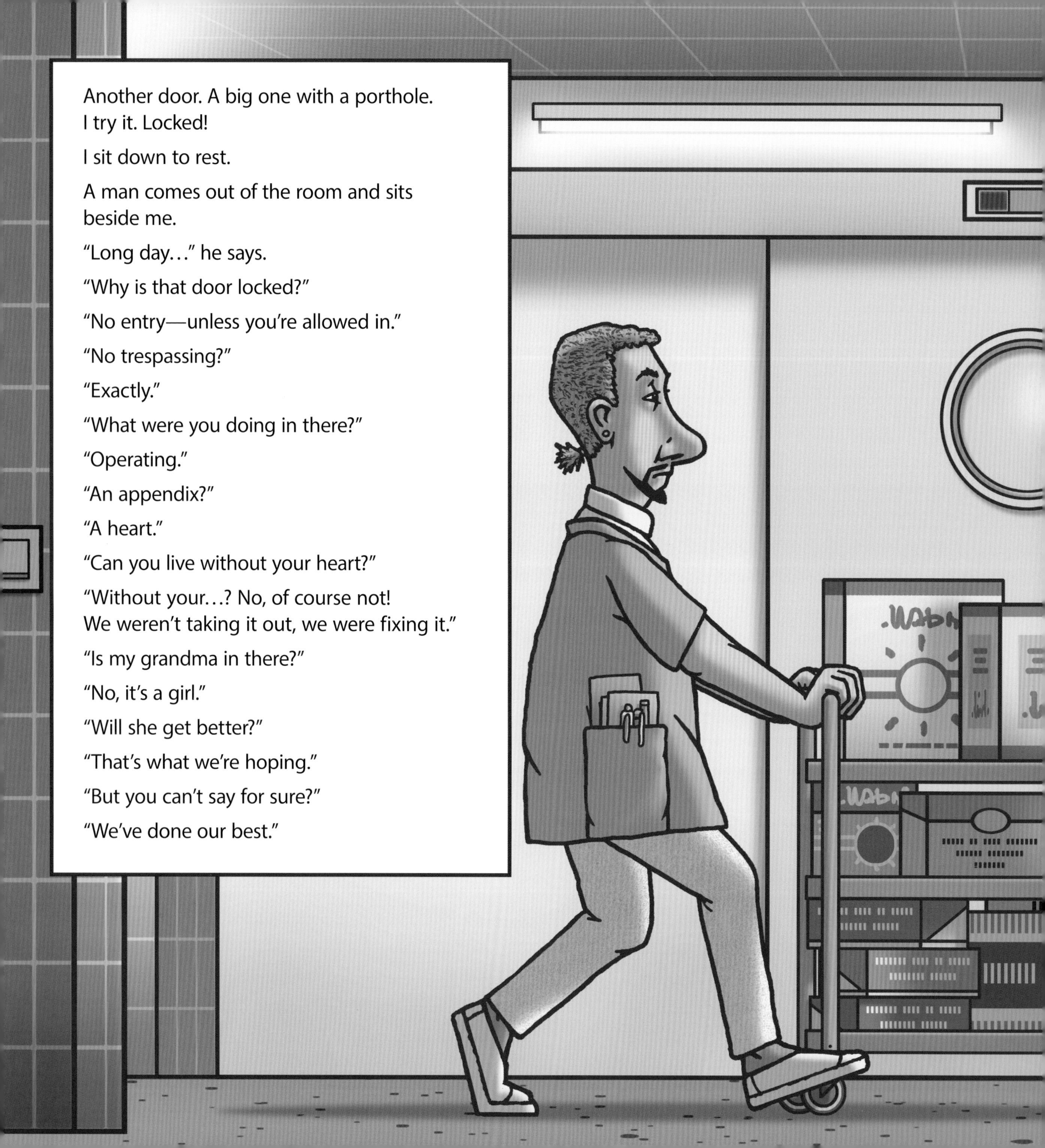
Another door. A big one with a porthole.
I try it. Locked!
I sit down to rest.
A man comes out of the room and sits beside me.
“Long day…” he says.
“Why is that door locked?”
“No entry—unless you’re allowed in.”
“No trespassing?”
“Exactly.”
“What were you doing in there?”
“Operating.”
“An appendix?”
“A heart.”
“Can you live without your heart?”
“Without your…? No, of course not!
We weren’t taking it out, we were fixing it.”
“Is my grandma in there?”
“No, it’s a girl.”
“Will she get better?”
“That’s what we’re hoping.”
“But you can’t say for sure?”
“We’ve done our best.”

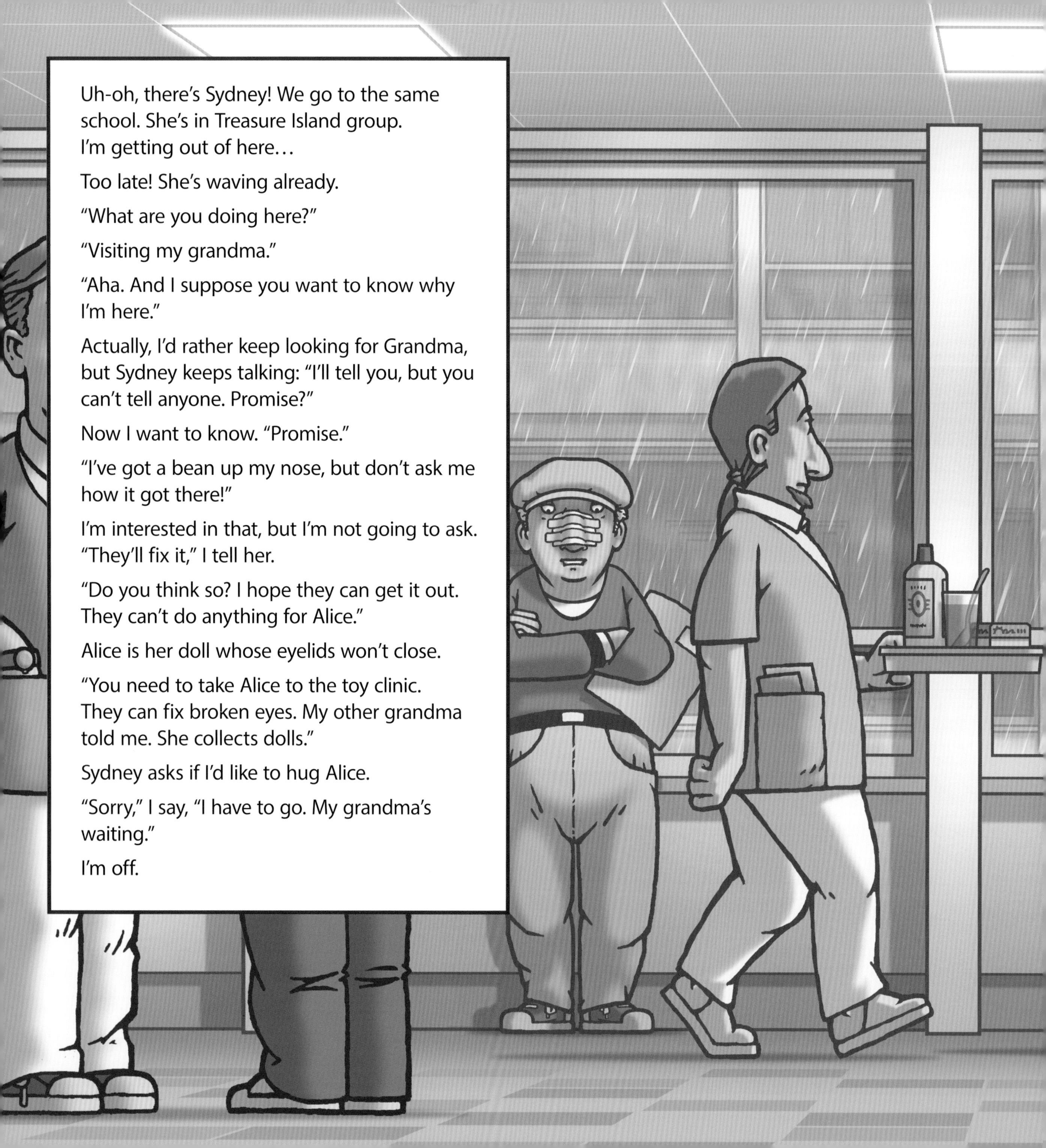

Uh-oh, there's Sydney! We go to the same school. She's in Treasure Island group. I'm getting out of here…

Too late! She's waving already.

"What are you doing here?"

"Visiting my grandma."

"Aha. And I suppose you want to know why I'm here."

Actually, I'd rather keep looking for Grandma, but Sydney keeps talking: "I'll tell you, but you can't tell anyone. Promise?"

Now I want to know. "Promise."

"I've got a bean up my nose, but don't ask me how it got there!"

I'm interested in that, but I'm not going to ask. "They'll fix it," I tell her.

"Do you think so? I hope they can get it out. They can't do anything for Alice."

Alice is her doll whose eyelids won't close.

"You need to take Alice to the toy clinic. They can fix broken eyes. My other grandma told me. She collects dolls."

Sydney asks if I'd like to hug Alice.

"Sorry," I say, "I have to go. My grandma's waiting."

I'm off.

Ah, an open door!
But no one’s there… On I go.

HOUSE

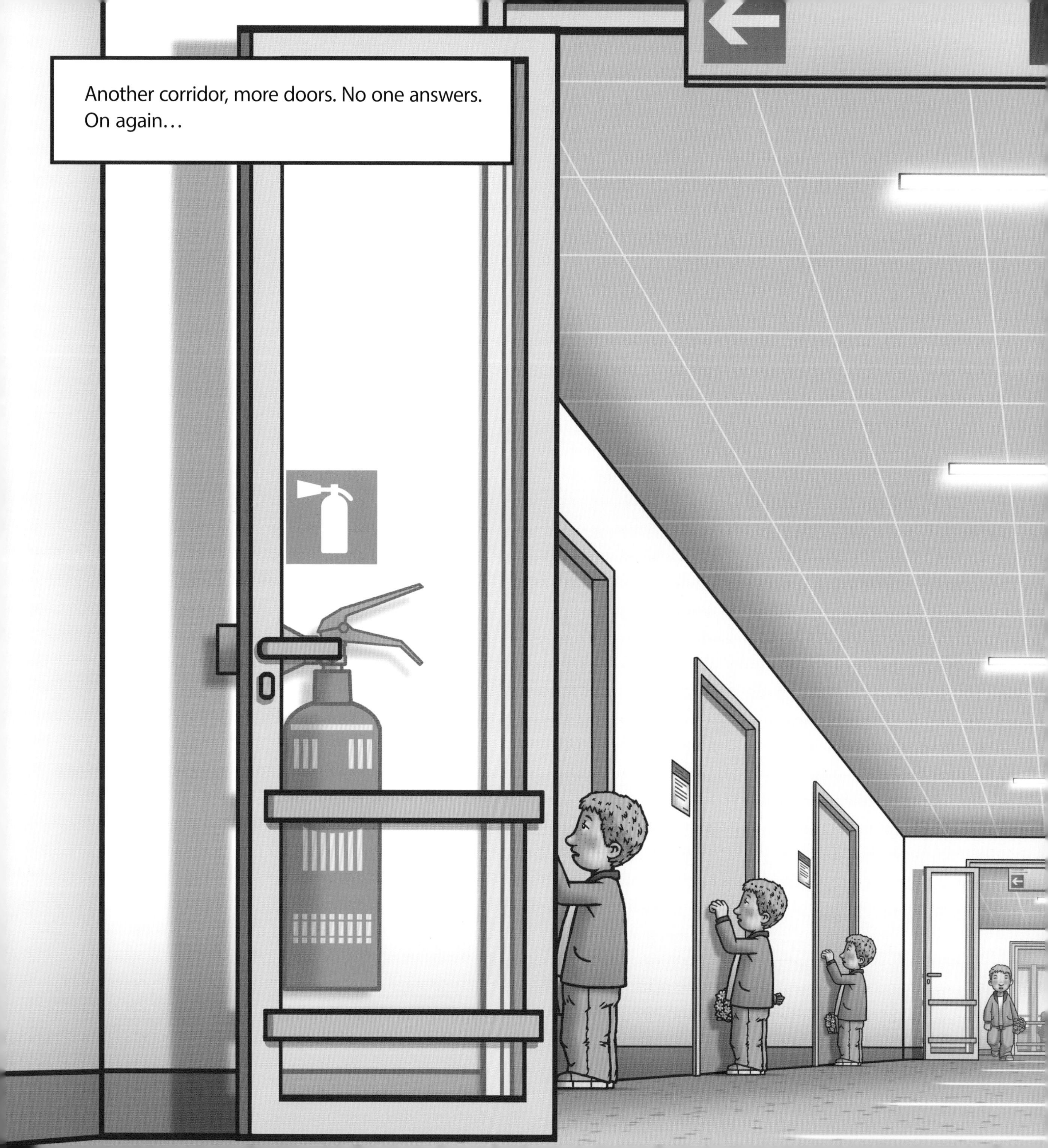
Another corridor, more doors. No one answers.
On again…

"Excuse me, young man, what are you doing here?"

"Looking for my grandma." I glance around, but no Grandma. "What are you doing here?" I ask.

"We look after people with stomach pain."

"I had a sore stomach and you didn't look after me!"

"It can't have been very serious then. Was it something you'd eaten?"

"Licorice. I ate the whole bag—most of it came up again afterwards."

"And you felt better?"

"Sort of… I don't like the smell of licorice any more. Dad says that will save us lots of money. He says we'll need it for my education."

"Right, well, we only see people with serious stomach pain—people with sweats and chills, who are really sore. If that happens, come here and we'll take care of you."

"What will you do?"

"That depends."

They tell me all the things it depends on, but I stop listening because I really want to find Grandma.

But next time I get a sore stomach I'll come straight here.

THE DIGESTIVE SYSTEM
LIVER
GALLBLADDER
DUODENUM
OESOPHAGUS
PANCREAS
STOMACH
PANCREATIC DUCT
COMMON BILE DUCT
LARGE INTESTINE
CAECUM
APPENDIX
RECTUM
ANUS
SMALL INTESTINE

No one down here, just a lot of pipes. I'm in the basement. A man glides up on an electric scooter. I'd like one of those.

"How did you get here?" he asks.

"From upstairs. I want to go back up."

"You're Henry who's visiting his grandma, right? They've been looking for you everywhere, young man. Hang on!" He talks into his phone, listens and then says: "Take the elevator to the fourth floor. A man called Harvey-James will be waiting to take you to your grandma."

I ask the scooter-man what he's doing in the basement.

"I'm downstairs control," he says. "I keep everything running—electricity, water, heating, laundry, all that."

"Henry, I presume?" says the man. "I'm Harvey-James from security and I'm here to take you to your grandma."
Finally!
04

On the way, he tells me what he does all day. “We make sure the hospital is safe for all the patients and staff. But we help with all kinds of things—like looking for patients who go missing, giving directions…”

"Do visitors go missing as well?" I ask.
"All the time," says Harvey-James. "But so far we've always found them."

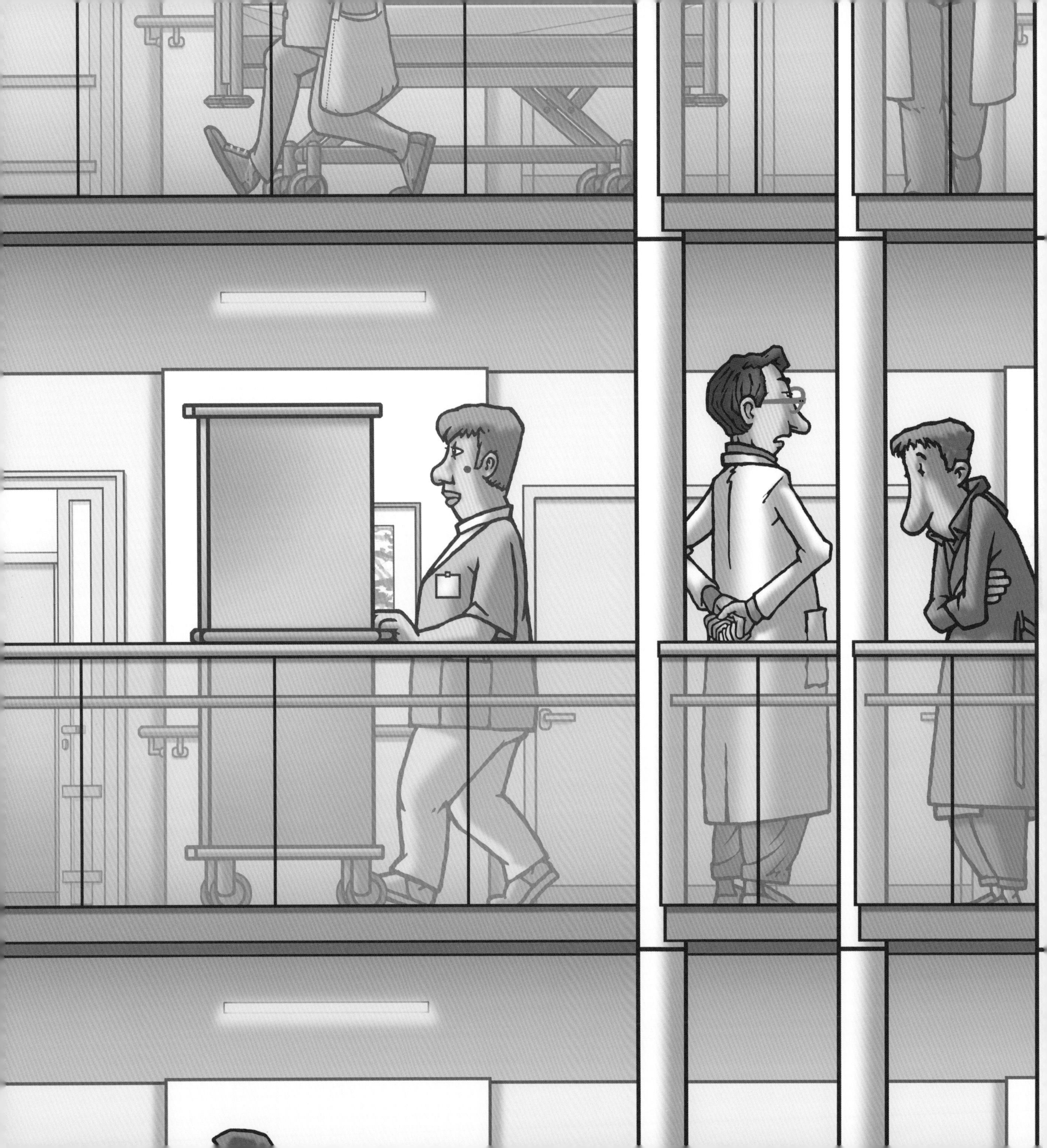

"Here we are," says Harvey-James. "I'll just let them know." He unhooks a phone from his belt. "Hello, switchboard? This is H-J!"
The phone crackles, then someone says: "This is J-K. What's the latest?"
"Mission accomplished. Errant person located. No sign of injury. Awaiting handover to grandmother."
The phone crackles some more, and the voice says: "Roger that."
33
34

35
WHo
42
MAN ORGAN
ANSPLANTATION
HANDLE WITH CARE

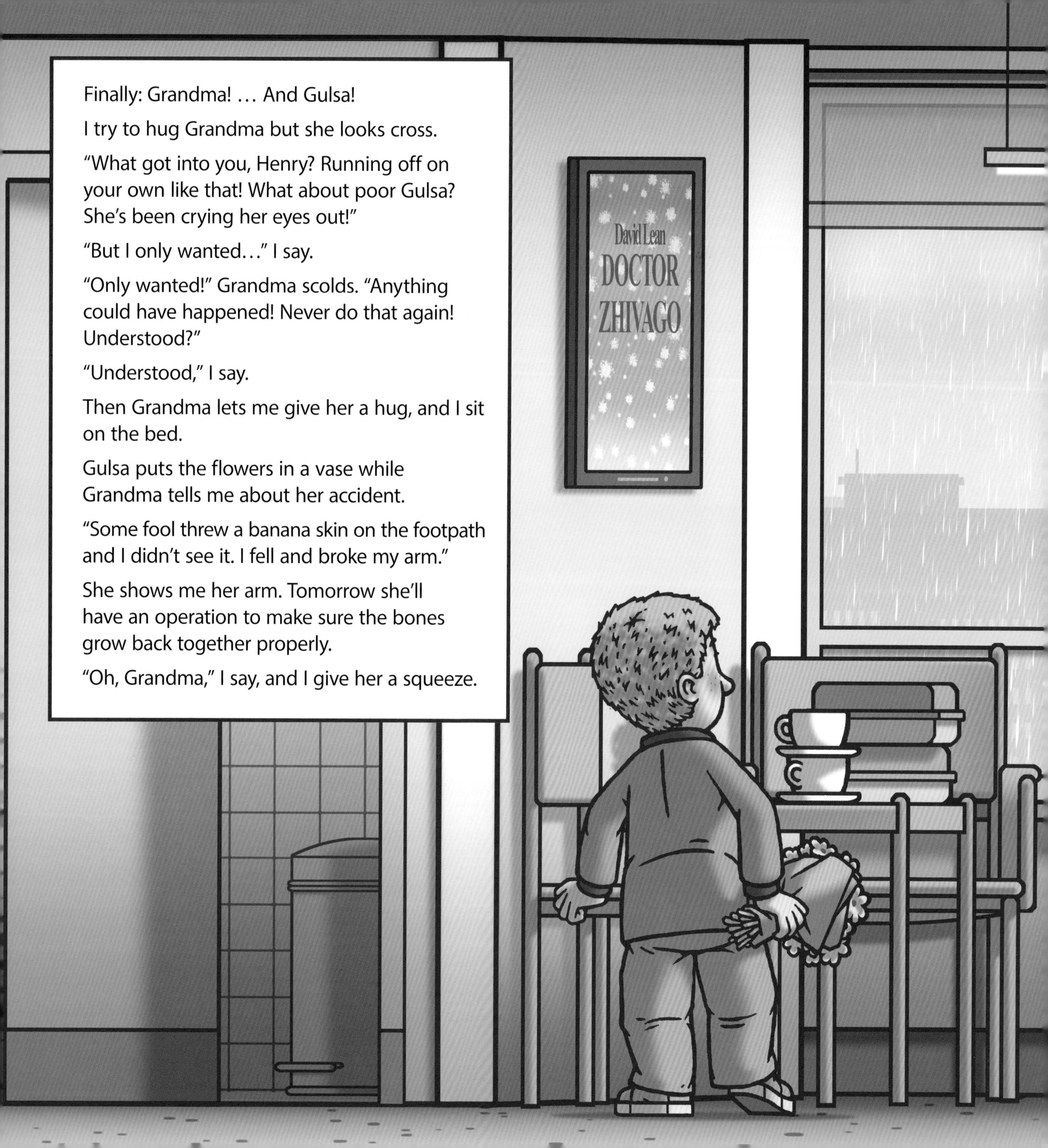
Finally: Grandma! … And Gulsa!
I try to hug Grandma but she looks cross.
“What got into you, Henry? Running off on your own like that! What about poor Gulsa? She’s been crying her eyes out!”
“But I only wanted…” I say.
“Only wanted!” Grandma scolds. “Anything could have happened! Never do that again! Understood?”
“Understood,” I say.
Then Grandma lets me give her a hug, and I sit on the bed.
Gulsa puts the flowers in a vase while Grandma tells me about her accident.
“Some fool threw a banana skin on the footpath and I didn’t see it. I fell and broke my arm.”
She shows me her arm. Tomorrow she’ll have an operation to make sure the bones grow back together properly.
“Oh, Grandma,” I say, and I give her a squeeze.
David Lean
DOCTOR
ZHIVAGO

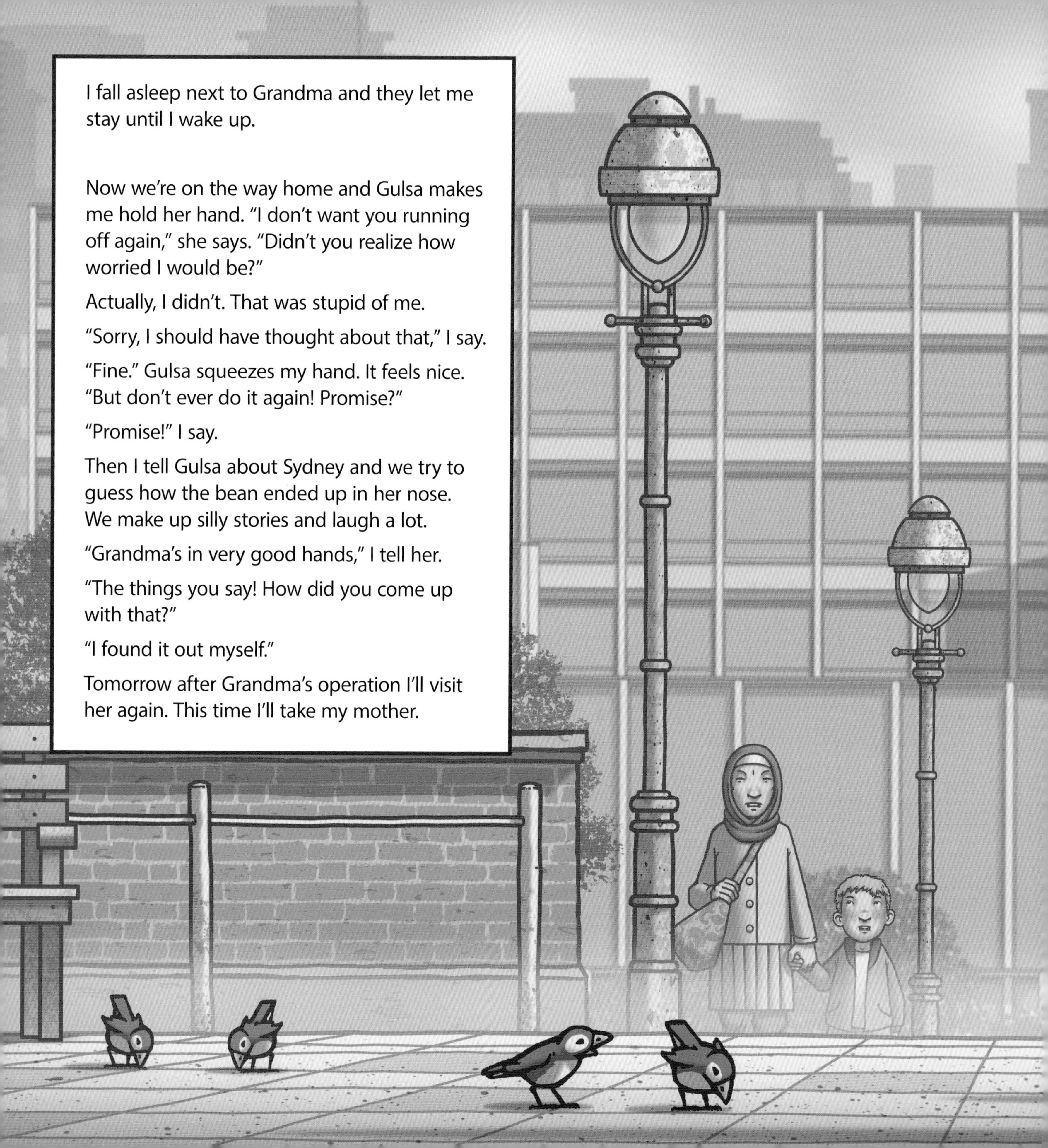
I fall asleep next to Grandma and they let me stay until I wake up.

Now we're on the way home and Gulsa makes me hold her hand. "I don't want you running off again," she says. "Didn't you realize how worried I would be?"

Actually, I didn't. That was stupid of me.

"Sorry, I should have thought about that," I say.

"Fine." Gulsa squeezes my hand. It feels nice. "But don't ever do it again! Promise?"

"Promise!" I say.

Then I tell Gulsa about Sydney and we try to guess how the bean ended up in her nose. We make up silly stories and laugh a lot.

"Grandma's in very good hands," I tell her.

"The things you say! How did you come up with that?"

"I found it out myself."

Tomorrow after Grandma's operation I'll visit her again. This time I'll take my mother.

This edition first published in 2017 by Gecko Press
PO Box 9335, Marion Square, Wellington 6141, New Zealand
info@geckopress.com

Distributed in the United States and Canada by Lerner Publishing Group, www.lernerbooks.com
Distributed in the United Kingdom by Bounce Sales and Marketing, www.bouncemarketing.co.uk
Distributed in Australia by Scholastic Australia, www.scholastic.com.au
Distributed in New Zealand by Upstart Distribution, www.upstartpress.co.nz

The translation of this book was supported by a grant from the Goethe-Institut which is funded by the German Ministry of Foreign Affairs.

Edited by Penelope Todd
Typesetting by Vida & Luke Kelly
Printed in China by Everbest Printing Co Ltd,
an accredited ISO 14001 & FSC certified printer

ISBN hardback: 978-1-776571-54-3
ISBN paperback: 978-1-776571-55-0

For more curiously good books, visit www.geckopress.com